BENNY BEAR GOES TO THE PARK: A COUNTING BOOK

By Akeishia J. Patterson, Ed.D

Illustrated By Ashley E. Johnson

This book belongs to:
____

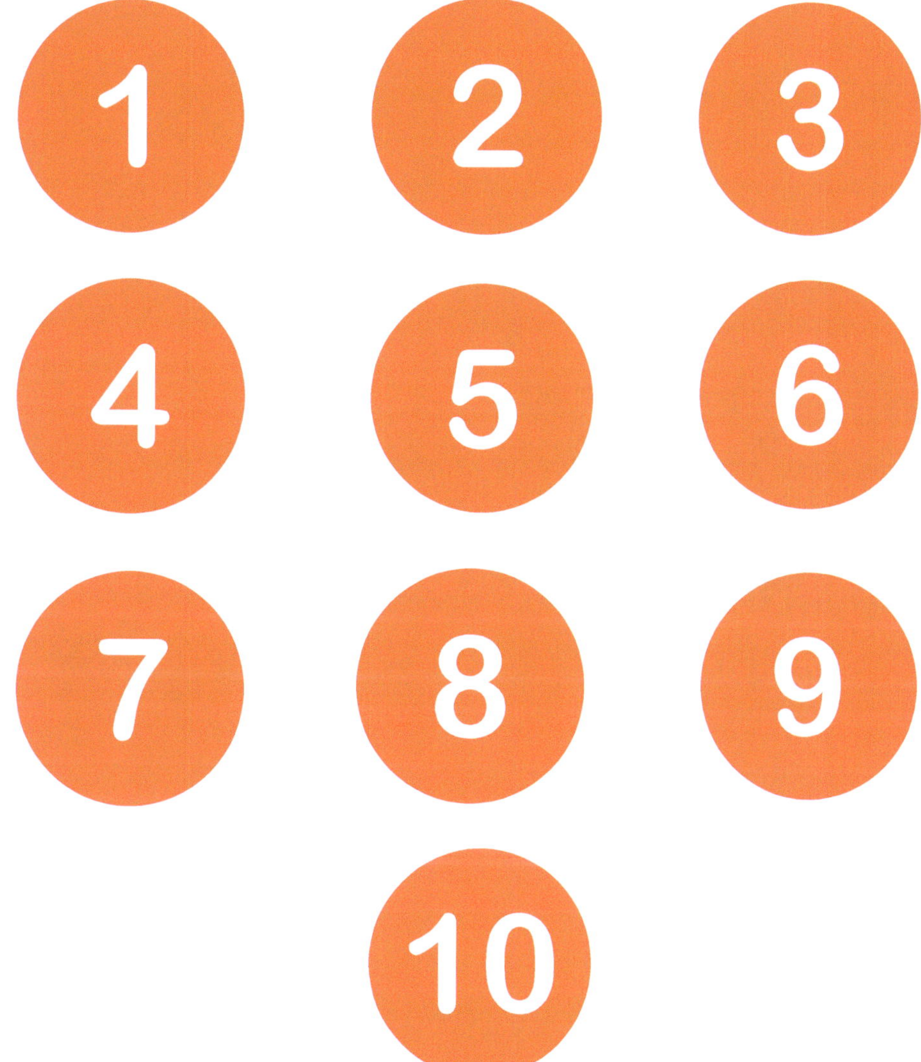

One sunny day Benny Bear
decided to go out

and he stumbled upon a park as he
was walking about.

He saw some amazing things as he
casually strolled through

and counted them one-by-one as
people usually do.

He counted **1** ant as it slowly crawled by

and **2** beautiful birds flying high in the sky.

He counted **3** flowers and stopped
to have a smell

and <u>4</u> tiny snails peeking out of
their shell.

He counted **5** children having lots of fun

and <u>6</u> yellow ducks swimming in a
nearby pond.

He counted **7** dogs running wild
and free

and **8** red apples dangling from a
tree.

He counted 9 bees buzzing
by their hive

and <u>10</u> colorful butterflies looking beautiful and alive.

Once he finished counting
everything in sight,

he headed back home to rest for
the night.

Knowledge Checkpoint

Use this section to discuss the book with your child.

1. Count from 1 to 10 with your child using the numbers on the following page.
2. Help your child identify numbers 1 through 10 on the following page.
3. Have your child tell some of the things Benny Bear counted in the park.
4. Have your child go back through the book and count the objects aloud on each page.

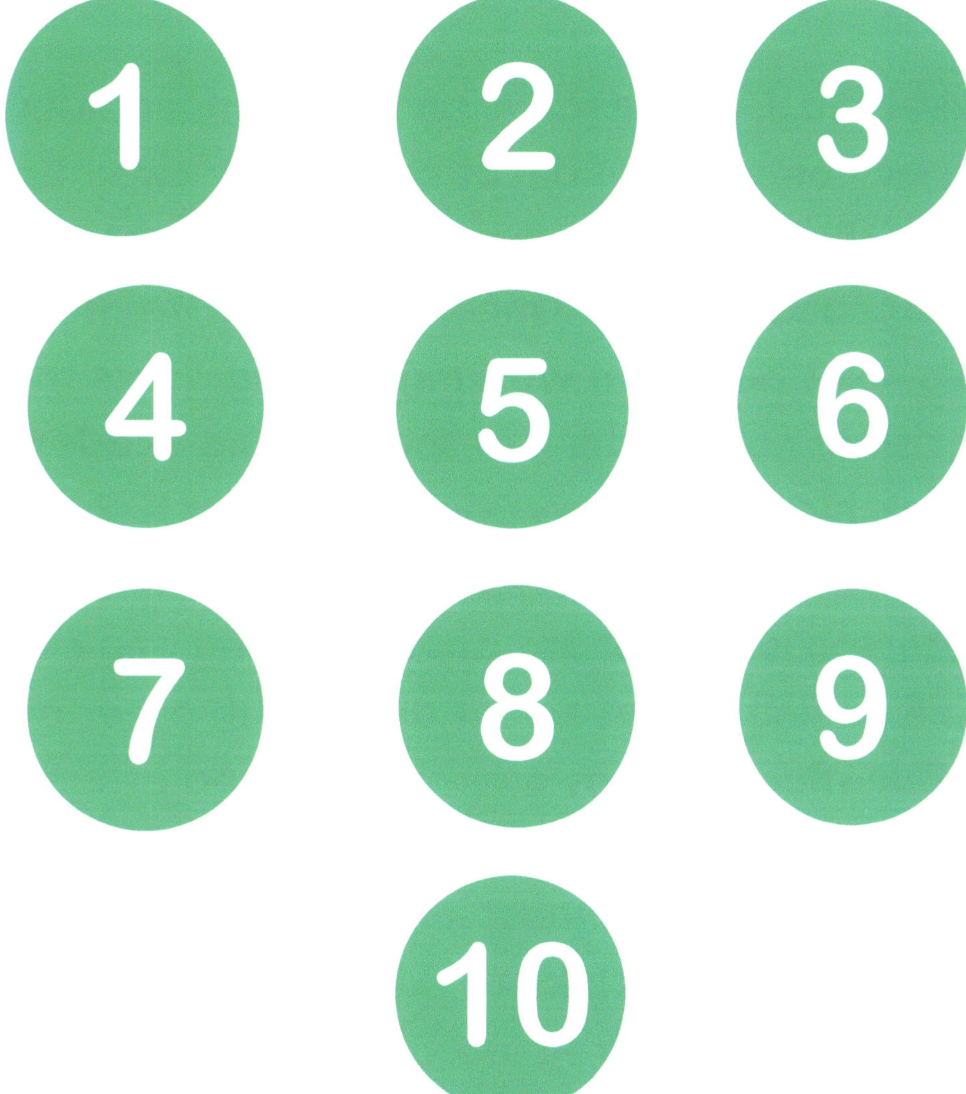

About the Author

Dr. Akeishia J. Patterson is an experienced educator that has been in the education field for close to two decades. She has always had a passion for teaching, learning, and reading. One of her favorite and most notable roles has been working with students that are at risk of not reaching or maintaining academic achievement in reading in grades K-2.

Dr. Patterson is passionate about reading and currently holds a Reading Endorsement along with other degrees in education. She has always dreamed of writing children's literature from an early age and believes reading is one of the most important and influential subjects taught to children. She thrives to not only write books that children learn from but enjoy reading as well.

About the Illustrator

Ashley E. Johnson is an illustrator, graphic designer, photographer, painter, and lover of art. She discovered her passion for art and drawing in the 4th grade while drawing an 18-wheeler in class and from there set her sights on becoming a part of the art world.

Ashley is an eccentric and fashionable artist that has sold artwork in exhibitions and created numerous pieces throughout her career. She draws her passion from the beautiful world around her and the people she meets. She credits her eye for photography to her dad and her keen eye for fashion to her mother. She has a degree in graphic design and firmly believes every illustration she creates will be just as exciting as the read.